W9-BHF-143

HOT WHEELS™

Cruise Control

By Myles Ryder

Illustrated by Dave White

SCHOLASTIC INC.

New York Toronto London Auckland Sydney
Mexico City New Delhi Hong Kong Buenos Aires

No part of this publication may be reproduced, stored in a
retrieval system, or transmitted in any form or by any means, electronic, mechanical,
photocopying, recording, or otherwise, without written permission of the copyright owner.
For information regarding permission, write to Scholastic Inc.,
Attention: Permissions Department, 557 Broadway, New York, NY 10012.

ISBN-13: 978-0-545-98928-2
ISBN-10: 0-545-98928-0

HOT WHEELS and associated trademarks and trade dress are owned by, and used
under license from Mattel, Inc. © 2008 Mattel, Inc. All Rights Reserved.

Published by Scholastic Inc. SCHOLASTIC and associated logos
are trademarks and/or registered trademarks of Scholastic Inc.

12 11 10 9 8 7 6 5 4   10 11 12/0

Printed in the U.S.A.   40
First printing, September 2008

Today is the big
race across the U.S.A.

The cars line up. The engines roar.

The fog lifts. Ready, set, RACE!

Golden Gate Bridge, California

The red car takes an early lead.

The road is dry. The sun is hot.

The yellow car needs more gas.

Look out for snakes!

Grand Canyon, Arizona

The cars are riding high.
The drivers do not look down.

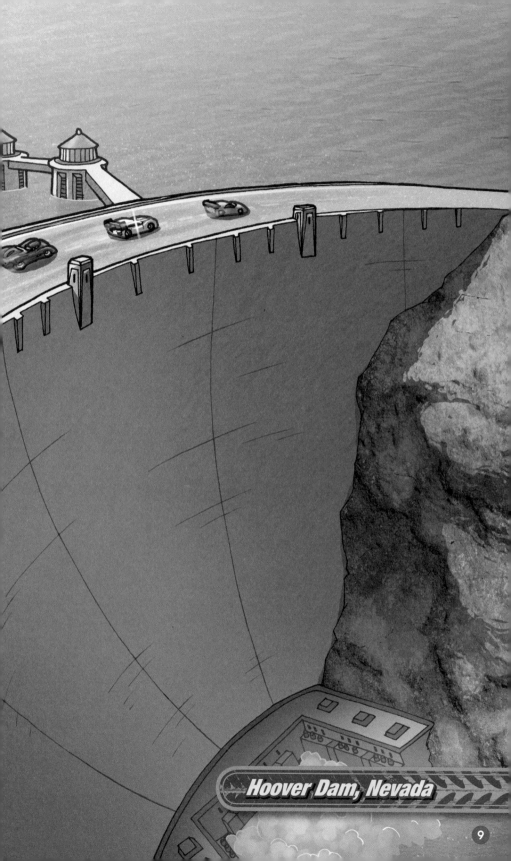

Hoover Dam, Nevada

Some roads are smooth.
Some roads are bumpy.

Look at the
faces in the rock!

Mount Rushmore, South Dakota

It is raining hard.
The blue car skids.
Water rises in the river.
The white car is stuck.

The cars zoom like rockets.

Get ready to blast off!

Cape Canaveral, Florida

The cars go over the hills.
Is that a bear?

The green car is in front.

Smoky Mountains, Tennessee

Horses have their own race.
Who is faster?
The car or the horse?

Welcome to the capital city!
The cherry trees are in bloom.

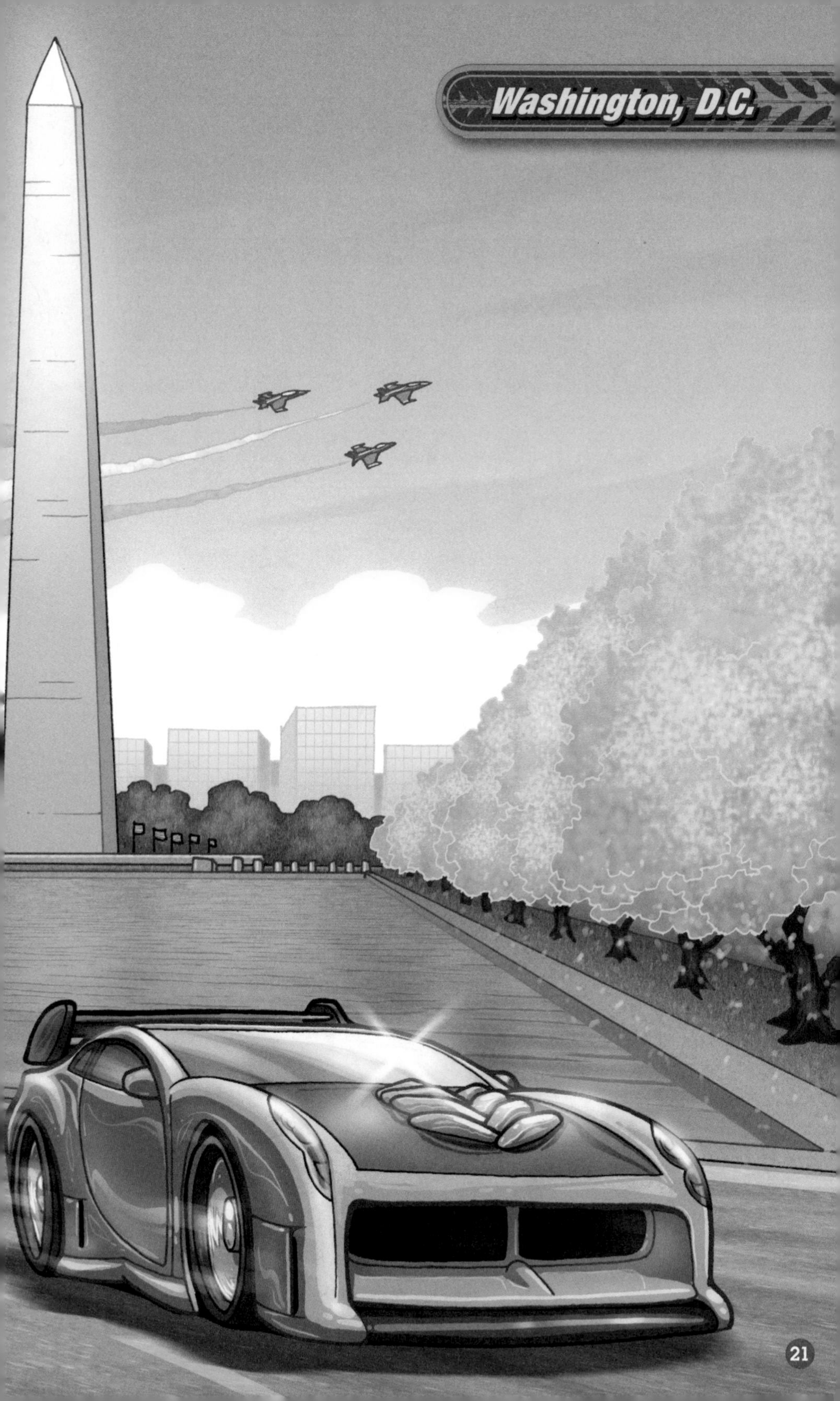
Washington, D.C.

Look at that sight.

And listen to that waterfall!

Niagara Falls, New York

The coast is rocky.
The ocean looks cold.

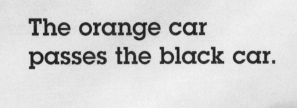

The orange car
passes the black car.

Its engine makes a noise.

Oh, no! The orange car spins off the road.

The black car blows a tire.
The blue car moves ahead.

Welcome to New York City.
We have a winner!

New York City, New York